P9-BYY-421
3 1257 01679 0957

YOUNG CAM JANSEN and the Pizza Shop Mystery

by David A. Adler

illustrated by Susanna Natti

PUFFIN BOOKS

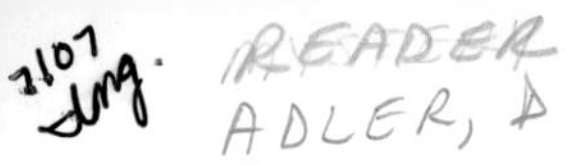

For Mom,
Happy *very* special birthday
—D. A.

To Lisa, Aron, Adam, and Sophie
—S. N.

PUFFIN BOOKS
Published by the Penguin Group
Penguin Putnam Books for Young Readers, 345 Hudson Street, New York, New York 10014, U.S.A.
Penguin Books Ltd, 27 Wrights Lane, London W8 5TZ, England
Penguin Books Australia Ltd, Ringwood, Victoria, Australia
Penguin Books Canada Ltd, 10 Alcorn Avenue, Toronto, Ontario, Canada M4V 3B2
Penguin Books (N.Z.) Ltd, 182-190 Wairau Road, Auckland 10, New Zealand

Penguin Books Ltd, Registered Offices: Harmondsworth, Middlesex, England

First published in the United States of America by Viking,
a division of Penguin Putnam Books for Young Readers, 2000
Published by Puffin Books, a division of Penguin Putnam Books for Young Readers, 2001

13 15 17 19 20 18 16 14 12

THE LIBRARY OF CONGRESS HAS CATALOGED THE VIKING EDITION AS FOLLOWS:
Adler, David A.
Young Cam Jansen and the pizza shop mystery / by David A. Adler ; illustrated by Susanna Natti.
p. cm. — [A Viking easy-to-read. Level 2]
Summary: When Cam, her friend Eric, and her father stop for pizza while they are at the mall,
Cam must rely on her photographic memory to locate her missing jacket.
ISBN 0-670-88861-3
[1. Memory—Fiction. 2. Mystery and detective stories.]
I. Natti, Susanna, ill. II. Title. III. Series.
PZ7.A2615Yt 2000 [Fic]—dc21 99-41979 CIP AC

Puffin Books ISBN 0-14-230020-9

Printed in China
Set in Bookman

Reading Level 2.0

CONTENTS

Cam Jansen has an amazing memory. Do you?

Look at this picture. Blink your eyes and say "Click!" Then turn to the last page of this book.

1. THE CROWDED MALL

“Stay with me.

Don’t get lost,”

Mr. Jansen told his daughter, Cam,

and her friend Eric Shelton.

It was late afternoon

on the first day of school.

Cam, Eric, and Mr. Jansen

were in the shopping mall.

Cam and Eric needed things for school.

The mall was crowded.

Mr. Jansen looked into

the stationery store.

It was filled with people buying

pens, pencils, crayons, notebooks,

and other things.

“Let’s eat first,” Mr. Jansen said.

“Then we’ll shop.”

Mr. Jansen looked around.

“Where should we eat?” he asked.

Cam closed her eyes.

She said, “Click!”

“I’m looking at the map we saw

when we came into the mall,” Cam said.

Her eyes were still closed.

Cam has an amazing memory.

She says, “It’s like a camera.

I have pictures in my head

of everything I've seen.

Click! is the sound my camera makes."

"We're near Mel's Pizza Shop," Cam said.

Cam's real name is Jennifer,

but because of her great memory

people started to call her "The Camera."

Soon "The Camera" became just "Cam."

Cam opened her eyes.

"There it is," she said. She pointed.

Mr. Jansen said, "Let's eat!"

2. LOTS OF TABLES, LOTS OF NOISE

A man in front of the pizza shop
called out, "Hi! I'm Mel.
Come in and eat the world's best pizza."
Cam, Eric, and Mr. Jansen went in.
There was a long line of people
waiting to buy pizza.

A boy in a yellow shirt

was carrying a tray.

On it were slices of pizza

and cups of soda.

A girl in a blue jacket rushed past him and

out of the shop.

A woman and two small boys

walked past him, too.

"Hey," the boy in the yellow shirt said

to one of the small boys.

"You knocked my tray.

Some soda spilled."

"I'm sorry," the small boy said.

Mr. Jansen told Cam and Eric,

"Please, get a table.

I'll wait in line."

Cam and Eric went to the back of the shop.

There were lots of tables.

There was lots of noise, too.

"Give me that!" a girl shouted

and grabbed a cup of soda from a boy.

"It's my soda!" the boy said.

He grabbed the cup

and soda spilled on him and the girl.

"Dana! Dana!" an old woman called out.

"Where are you?"

The woman was holding a tray

with two slices of pizza

and two cups of soda on it.

"There's an empty table," Cam said.

Cam and Eric hurried to it.

Cam put her jacket over the back of a chair.

"I'll tell Dad where we're sitting," Cam said.

Cam went to the front of the shop.

Eric followed her.

It was almost Mr. Jansen's turn

to buy pizza.

Cam told her father,

"We found a table in the back."

"Just sit there and wait for me,"

Mr. Jansen said. "I'll find you."

Then he asked, "What do you want to drink?"

"Apple juice," Cam told him.

"I want apple juice, too," Eric said.

Cam turned and saw Eric.

"If you're here," she asked,

"who is watching our table?"

Eric said, "Your jacket is."

Cam hurried to the back

of the pizza shop.

Eric followed her.

They couldn't find their table

and they couldn't find Cam's jacket.

3. YOU COULD BE WRONG!

"Here's the pizza and apple juice,"

Mr. Jansen said. "Where do we sit?"

Cam closed her eyes and said, "Click!"

Then she said, "I know where our table is."

Cam opened her eyes.

She led Eric and her father to a table.

There was a tray with two slices of pizza

and two cups of soda on the table.

"Someone else is sitting here," Eric said.

No one was sitting at the next table.

"Let's just sit here," Mr. Jansen said.

"Let's eat before the pizza gets cold."

They sat at the next table.

Eric and Mr. Jansen started to eat.

Cam didn't.

She closed her eyes and said, "Click!"

"I'm sure that's our table," Cam said.

"You know," Eric said. "You could be wrong."

Cam said, "Click!" again.

"I'm not wrong," she said.

"Our table was in the corner.

It was under the light."

Cam opened her eyes.

"And my jacket," she said,

"was on that chair." She pointed.

"Your jacket!" Mr. Jansen said.

Mr. Jansen got up.

"I left it right there," Cam told her father.

Mr. Jansen looked under the chair

and the table.

Cam, Eric, and Mr. Jansen

walked from table to table.

They looked at the backs of every chair

and under every table.

"It's lost," Mr. Jansen told Cam.

"Your jacket is lost."

4. CLICK! CLICK! CLICK!

Cam and Eric followed Mr. Jansen
to the front of the shop.
"My daughter put her jacket
over the back of a chair,"
Mr. Jansen told Mel.
"Now it's gone."
"I'll find it," Mel said.
He led Cam, Eric, and Mr. Jansen
behind the counter to a big box.

“Your jacket is in there,” Mel said.

“Everything we find is in that box.”

There were hats, gloves, scarves,

a sneaker, and a baby shoe in the box.

But not Cam’s jacket.

“It’s not here,” Cam told Mel.

“Maybe you left it in your car,” Mel said.

“Or maybe you left it at school.”

“No,” Cam said. “I know where I left it.”

She led everyone back to the table.

She said, "I left it right here."

Eric was still hungry.

He picked up his half-eaten slice of pizza.

"Hey, this is cold," he said.

"Of course it's cold," Mel said.

"You left it there too long."

Cam looked at Eric.

Then she looked at the next table.

The tray with pizza

and cups of soda was still there.

"That's it!" Cam said.

Click! Click! Click!

"What is she doing?" Mel asked.

"Sh," Eric whispered.

"Cam is looking at something."

"No, she's not," Mel said.

"Her eyes are closed."

Mr. Jansen told Mel about Cam's amazing memory.

Then Cam opened her eyes and said,

"An old woman in a yellow dress

took my jacket.

She thought it was Dana's."

"She did?" Mel asked.

"Dana has long brown hair," Cam said.

"She's wearing a blue jacket,

jeans, and red sneakers."

"But how do you know?" Mel asked.

"When I said 'Click!' I remembered

that when we came into the shop

a girl wearing a blue jacket rushed past us."

"I think I remember her, too,"

Mr. Jansen said.

"And then," Cam said,

"when we were looking for a table,

the woman in the yellow dress

called out, 'Dana! Dana!'

She was holding a tray

with two slices of pizza and two cups of soda."
Eric said, "And she left it on our table."
"Yes," Cam said. "She saw my blue jacket
and thought it was Dana's.
When she couldn't find her,
she left the pizza, took the blue jacket,
and went looking for Dana."
Mel said, "You do have an amazing memory.
I'll bet you have the best memory in the world."

5. THE VERY, VERY BEST

Cam hurried to the front of the shop.

She walked to the center of the mall

and looked for the woman.

Eric, Mr. Jansen, and Mel followed Cam

and looked, too.

"Is that her?" Mel asked and pointed.

"No," Cam told him.

"Is that her?" Mel asked again and pointed.

"No," Cam told him.

“There they are,” Mr. Jansen said.

He ran to an old woman and a girl.

Cam, Eric, and Mel followed him.

“I’m Mel,” Mel said, “from Mel’s Pizza Shop.”

“I’m Sara and I’m sorry,” the woman told him.

“I took this jacket by mistake.”

She gave a blue jacket to Mel.

Mel gave it to Cam.

Dana said, “I ran out of the pizza shop

to look for my grandma.”

Sara said, "And I took a jacket. I thought it was Dana's. Then I went looking for her."

"I know," Mel said and pointed to Cam. "Cam told me."

"She did?" Sara asked. "But how did she know?"

Mel said, "Cam has a camera in her head."

Sara and Dana looked at Cam.

Dana said, "I don't see a camera. I just see red hair and freckles."

"It's her memory," Mr. Jansen explained.

"Her memory is like a camera."

"Oh," Sara and Dana said.

"I'm just glad you found each other,"

Mel told Sara and Dana.

"And I'm glad I found you."

Mel brought them back to his shop.

He gave them all fresh slices of pizza.

"This pizza is good," Cam said.

Eric, Dana, Sara, and Mr. Jansen said,

"It's very good."

"Of course it is," Mel said.

"It's the best pizza in the world —

the very, very best."

A Cam Jansen Memory Game

Take another look at the picture on page 4.

Study it.

Blink your eyes and say, "Click!"

Then turn back to this page

and answer these questions:

1. What color is Mr. Jansen's jacket?
2. Is Eric wearing a jacket?
3. Is Cam wearing a jacket?
4. Are there more than 10 people in the picture?
5. What is in Mr. Jansen's hand?